Marissa Moss

Want to Play?

Houghton Mifflin Company
Boston 1990

For Shelah, Steven, and Elise

Library of Congress Cataloging-in-Publication Data

Moss, Marissa.
  Want to play? / Marissa Moss.
    p. cm.
  Summary: Two toddlers experience the frustrations of learning to
share their toys.
  ISBN 0-395-52022-3
  [1. Play—Fiction. 2. Sharing—Fiction.] I. Title.
PZ7.M8535Wan   1990   89-24504
[E]—dc20   CIP
               AC

Printed in the United States of America

WOZ 10 9 8 7 6 5 4 3 2 1

Want to Play?

"Don't follow me!" said Jonas.

"I'm not," said Frieda. "I'm just going the same way."

"Hey, that's mine!" yelled Jonas.

"Leave my stuff alone," said Jonas.

"Put that down!" growled Jonas.

"I just want to play," said Frieda.

"Well, I don't," said Jonas.

"Want to play catch?" asked Frieda.

"No," said Jonas, "I don't."

"What's that?" asked Jonas.
"A feather," said Frieda.

"Want to trade?" asked Jonas.

"No, thanks," said Frieda.

"I'm playing."